The Twelve Days of Murder

by
Koh Wiirkir

A Note From the Author:

The Twelve Days of Murder was written as a bit of fun. Although I had other books under contract that needed to be written, I chose to give myself, and hopefully some of you, a little comic relief. I stole the idea from a co-worker. We were both trying to write novels for a writing contest. She said she wanted to write a murder mystery with this store as the backdrop. I don't want to give out her name but told her, "Jody, that is a great idea." It was good enough for me to steal. And by the way, Jody, I stole your lunch yesterday, too.

As I tossed around the idea, many of you pitched in ideas. Kolby and I even discussed how he would expire. Drew's murder, however, was a labor of love on my part. Raw, Ro! Just kidding, Drew. Since I knew Cheryl the best, she became my lead character.

Both Pat and Frank were the two biggest encouragements as I got stalled on the project. The three of us decided it needed to be a fund raiser for the Sunshine Club. In other words, the proceeds from your purchase go to aid in collectively bringing a little sunshine into the lives of our co-workers in their troublesome moments.

The Twelve Days of Murder is a mystery. Try to guess who the killer is. It will be fun. It is also a horror book. I had twelve bestsellers in the Children's market writing kid's horror stories. It is what I do best. Lastly, it is a parody book. I played it for laughs by drawing caricatures of all you with words. I am an equal opportunity punster so don't get your panties in

towards the stockroom before a black Infinity scarf was pulled tight around her neck.

THE END
or is it just the beginning?

Who do you think did it? There are only a few possibilities. Or was there more than one killer? And what about those who were not scheduled for the evening? How did the killer know that Kellie had made up a game based on the song even before she announced it?

corner of the back hall, where Chad grabbed a few items for the new candy display. Cheryl told him about more of the killings. Some amused him and a few others were sad. Eric's demise put a smile on his face.

Once they reached the end of the hall by the candy store room, the Candyman was stacking his dolly high with the new Death by Chocolate candy boxes. As he went to move it, the boxes teetered, wobbled and then the top one fell. The exciting new candy box thudded to the ground and the one pound boxes poured out of the carton. The top box broke open and there before them all was the tantalizingly sweet chocolates. The aroma was hypnotic.

"So this is Death By Chocolate?" Chad asked.

"It looks like we can't sell this box. Would you like one?"

Chad said, "Sure," and grabbed a piece.

"Don't eat it!" Cheryl screamed but her voice couldn't be heard over the speakers above as Pat made an announcement about a freak Winter storm heading their way. Cheryl was too far away to stop Chad as he popped it in his mouth.

Then something black moved in the corner of her eye. Cheryl spun her head quickly but it had already disappeared into the candy storage room. She wasn't sure what it was but she thought she saw a misty, dark figure in a hood and a robe wearing a black Infinity scarf step into the doorway of the candy store room. Cheryl heard a soft chuckle come from the Candyman and a faint cackle from the misty figure in black. She knew the voice but she couldn't believe who it belonged to. Cheryl took two steps

"What happened to you, Rich? Were you moved by the Christmas spirit?"

"I was moved by the Spirit," Rich answered as he folded his arms over his chest, miraculously changed colors like a chameleon and faded into the background as a squirrel peaked from under his pant leg.

"Now onto the hot topics. Most of you have seen the ads all over TV for the new candy that is taking the nation by storm. We got it in late yesterday. Chad is putting up the display now and Susanna and her team are getting it out right away. I wanted to have everyone taste it but Faithanne informed me that it is $85 a pound. Susanna was willing to pay for it out of her pocket but I couldn't allow her to do that. You're too good to us all, Susanna. It isn't in the budget obviously but Mr. B has agreed to give a sampler box to anyone who wins tonight's game. Kellie has got a great game for us to play. Tell them about it, Kellie," Pat finished.

"I call it the Twelve Days of Christmas. All you have to do is find, hear, locate or witness a clue that goes along with one of the lines from the song, The Twelve Days of Christmas. Here are the game cards. Make sure your other department members get a copy," Kellie told them and she passed out the cards.

Cheryl grew a little faint but rationalized that this had to be a coincidence. Once the meeting ended she caught up to Chad and started telling him about her dream. He laughed at the part with Adam in the crock pot and Sean eating the carrots but didn't think it was anymore than a dream. They rounded the

Cheryl's near trance after her terrible nightmare. She rubbed her face and stood up. The store friends gathered their belongings and headed to their cars for the evening and overnight at the Big B.

Cheryl had a new perspective on the co-workers she bumped into. She was genuinely glad to see them and gave out as many hugs as she could possibly give. As she passed Davey on the escalator, she yelled out, "You're the man, Davey!" Davey looked at her and wondered what that meant but inwardly agreed with her statement. She was headed back to Chad's Visuals office when Pat called for a meeting in Furniture.

Once everyone had settled in, the Store Manager began to speak, "I want to thank everyone who volunteered for this long night. Let me begin by saying that we had a fantastic day with charge applications yesterday. Let me read the list:

Judy in Customer service, amazing, one in Customer Service?

Rich, from Housewares,
Rich,
Rich,
Rich,
Rich,
Shelley,
Rich,
Rich,
Rich,
Connie,
The Candyman,
Rich,
Rich.

idea what is going on. I was never in that cool, pleasant room filled with wonderful chocolates. Who is this woman in black that everyone is talking about?"

"I know who it is," said Cheryl. "I figured it out hours ago. It is none other than..." Suddenly two hands gripped her throat and screamed into her ear.

Cheryl could hear a voice behind her. Sean was screaming her name. Was she the next one? Was he accusing her of being the woman in black. Was Sean the woman in black? "Cheryl, Cheryl! Wake up! We have to be at the store in twenty minutes and it is starting to snow. Let's go."

"What? What's that? Oh, this is wonderful. It wasn't real. It was only a dream. We're all still alive!" Dave, Leah, Sean, Adam and Kate looked at Cheryl with complete surprise. Of course, it wasn't the first time they had looked at her in complete surprise.

"What are you talking about, Cheryl? Adam may not be a great cook but I don't think his turkey was that bad," Kate said.

"No, no. I had the most horrible dream. Someone was killing people in the store throughout the night," Cheryl told them. "It was a real nightmare. It was horrible. Just remind me never to drink cheap vodka with the turkey ever again. It must have been tainted with radiation from Chernobyl or Tim. Adam you were decapitated and your head was cooked in a crock pot," Cheryl went on.

"Remember, Adam, live by crock-pot, die by crock-pot," Dave joked. The laughter helped to break

Oh my, I can't believe YOU did this to me," he remarked as he stared into the crowd that pressed close eager to hear his accusation. No one was sure exactly who it was that he was looking towards. He bolted to a standing position and took a step towards the group of co-workers. Chad raised his hand slowly and his finger extended as he said, "It was..." At that moment a blue, Colorsplash ceramic coated, Santoku knife came out the crowd and embedded itself in Chad's throat. The mysterious woman in black and the mastermind of the Twelve Days of Murder had killed off the last witness except for one—the nefarious but lovable Candyman.

The co-workers looked around. The mild-mannered, often quiet and reserved purveyor of edible delights was gone but the actual lady in black, the thrower of the knife, was obviously still amongst them. Undiscovered and undetected. Ready to strike again.

All the heads turned to the escalator. There was pounding at the front door to the store. It sounded like drums beating on the glass. The police were finally there but it was too late.

"That's it. I won. I got all twelve in Kellie's game," said Michael. A few of the co-workers spun towards him and considered that one more death might be in order.

"Won what?" said Janine as she stepped from the crowd. The co-workers looked at her with suspicion for she had been mysteriously missing for most of the night. "Wait a second, I was locked up, tied up and gagged inside the Handbags storage area. Buried under a pile of faux leather purses. I have no

Chad protested as he attempted to raise his body from the floor. Frank placed his foot on Chad's chest and pushed him back.

"I'm willing to listen to your story. What happened, Chad?" Frank said.

"The last thing I remember was trying to get a display ready for Susanna and Faithanne. I had gone back to the room where they keep the candy. As I got there, the Candyman, was moving a stack of boxes and the top one fell. It spilled pieces of candy everywhere. I was assisting him in picking it up. It was something new called Death By Chocolate. The Candyman insisted that I try one since the box was open.

"I took a bite. Man it was good. So, I had another. The next thing I knew my head was spinning. The Candyman helped me into that nice cool room where they keep all the candy. I sat down because I was growing weaker by the second. I was in some kind of a trance. I had no will to fight the suggestions being made to me by an ethereal, hypnotic voice. The last thing I remember was a figure in a black hood and long black robe, wearing a black Infinity Scarf or maybe a Figure 8 Scarf or possibly an Eternity Scarf. It was a woman's voice. She spoke to me in a hypnotic tone about killing people. I was to fake my own death then attack Drew and Kolby. I don't remember much after that."

"Who was the woman?" Pat asked.

"I can't be sure. I never saw her face. I knew the voice but I was still dizzy from the chocolate. It had to be a manager or a lead. I just know it was a woman. Wait a second, I remember the voice now.

handsome face, he slowly came to his senses and stared at everyone. He was surprised to see his co-workers standing over him. Clyde said to him, "How could you have killed all these co-workers?"

The killer blinked again and fell unconscious. They wouldn't have their answers yet. Clyde stood. "It was the perfect plan. He had us believing he was already dead but how did he pull it off?"

Brooke stepped forward and spoke with tears welling in her eyes, "Last Halloween, he asked me to create a mask of his face. I never saw it on him but I bet that is what is over a mannequin's head in the freight elevator, on top of the pear tree. But I can't believe Chad would do this." She broke into tears as Kamarki, Chase, Waylon and Tyler moved in to console her.

"I want to know why? Wake him up again Clyde?" said Pat as she stood with her hands on her hips. She was pissed and everyone knew it. No one wanted to get Pat pissed. No one. The second glass of water brought Chad around a second time.

"Where am I?" Chad asked.

"You are in our custody. You have killed many co-workers tonight. You'll get the chair for this," Clyde said.

"And I have just the one. It is a leather recliner with a heated lower lumbar cushion and an attached refrigerator. The sign on it says 'Crazy Prices.' It says that because you would be crazy not to buy it," said Garry.

"I don't mean that kind of chair. I mean the electric chair," Clyde corrected.

"What did I do? I don't remember a thing,"

Chapter 12: Twelve Coppers Drumming

The store breathed a sigh of relief. The dastardly killer was caught before he could do another villainous act. Clyde rolled the unconscious figure over. Everyone gasp again, because that is what people do at the moment of climax in any good book. This couldn't be the killer. They all thought that he was dead. They thought he was a victim. How could he have pulled it off? Clyde asked for a glass of cold water to splash on the killers face to bring him to.

The cool refreshing water was slow to come because the fountain slowed to a trickle when someone flushed the toilet in the ladie's room. Once the almost cool water hit the killer's ruggedly

Dave tripped and went flying into the Clearance table. Items flew across the store. The killer headed towards the Courtesy Counter.

The killer had made one miscalculation, he didn't see Kaylee who was carrying the change for the registers but she saw him. Kaylee ran towards the killer, leaped like a hard muscled gazelle on one couch in the Furniture clearance section priced at 50% off the lowest ticketed price, springing herself to the back of another and finally leaping ten feet in the air like a crouching tiger--hidden bitch, she brought twenty pounds of rolled pennies, nickels and quarters, but certainly not any dimes because the Big B didn't do dimes, down on the head of the killer. He crashed to the floor face down as Judy straddled his back to keep the villain in place with her shapely and sexy legs. Unknown to all, Judy was a former FBI agent sent in to infiltrate the store to nab an infamous jewelry thief that had burgled the store months before. She had her suspicions that there was a secret wanderer in the store as well. Wandering was a crime against mankind.

Clyde arrived a minute later and rolled the killer over. Everyone gasped in surprise at his identity.

hours, she found it helped to focus on the precious children of the world. Betty walked the toy aisles then decided to check the stock in the storeroom. She flipped on the switch but the lights flickered before going black. She tried again. Nothing happened. She heard Nancy calling her name. She turned to open the door and let Nancy in when a figure hiding behind the luggage raced towards her, running her through with a well waxed pipe broken from one of the children's clothing racks.

Nancy threw the door open in enough time to see the killer and watch Betty stumble backwards before falling. Nancy had a choice, chase down the killer or help her friend. She looked at Betty who croaked out, "It don't matter a hill of beans what happens to me. Go after that killer, Nancy. Do it for the children." Then Betty expired like the Stars and Moons cookies left over from the year before.

Nancy screamed and ran towards the figure moving out the door into Housewares. The killer was running like an NFL running back but so was Nancy. Nancy was yelling for someone to stop the man in black. Dave was looking for Johnny Cash and wondering why in the world he was in the store. However, Cheryl saw the figure running in her immediate direction. She crouched to make a hard body tackle. The killer grabbed a clock as he ran by and hurled it at Cheryl. She raised her arms to block the clock and missed the opportunity to bring the killer down, which was good for him for she would have destroyed him. He ran through the luggage tossing a 21" London Fog four-wheel spinner marked 50% off the lowest ticketed price in Dave's way.

that made people crazy if they didn't buy the items, would drive shoppers to the door even after the big snow storm.

She divided up the remaining workers to cover the various departments and instructed them to straighten things up but not to disturb the deceased co-workers then added, "If there are blood splatters on the clothes or other merchandise, throw it in bags. We will put it out later when our stock is low. Now, get to your departments. And by the way, since we are short handed we need everyone to work until close tonight. And be sure to take your two meal breaks."

The two playas, Karmarki and Chase would be split up. Dan was handling curtains and Nancy with Mary Ellen had gifts. Justin and Chase were sent to Accessories. Karmarki would go to Misses. He felt comfortable there. Since he was part of the Playa's Club, he knew he could outsell the former co-workers. All he had to do was smile and suggest a few extra items. Besides that hot new girl, Tori, would be working there. He would shine as only a playa could. Betty agreed to go to toys to cover that department.

Toys wouldn't be a problem for Betty. Nancy had agreed to come help her but wanted to freshen up first. Betty felt a need to familiarize herself with all the toys now that Gretchen and her team had gone to that big bassinet in the sky. She would do her best to make sure children got the toys they wanted in order to make Christmas better for the world. That was the way Betty lived her life. She wanted to make it better for others. After going without sleep the last few meandered behind him. "We can't protect these people if they don't stay together." Clyde stood and snatched one of Kellie's Twelve Days of Christmas game cards off of her counter. "According to this, we have pipers and drummers to go. I don't know what that means but I do know the cops will be here in less than two hours. The killer will have to work fast to get in the last two.

Michael and Kenny strolled up behind the two, scratching off one more on their game cards. Then they took the escalator back upstairs after stepping over the freshly dead body. Frank and Clyde followed. They had to give the bad news to the remaining co-workers. By this time, the group was weary of bad news. Most yawned when they heard it, rolled over and went back to sleep. Except for the remaining members of Eric's department. They argued over who most deserved to be the new manager. Larry and Shelley began to throw blows at one another while they tumbled to the floor tossing jabs at the other's head. Shelley got in a few good punches to Larry's kidney before her next punch bloodied his nose. It would be a battle to see who came out on top. But Shelley liked it on top.

It was quiet for the next hour. When the clock struck five, Val announced that it was time to get up. The co-workers grumbled. They wanted to know why they had to wake up. Val gave them the good news that the storm had stopped, the parking lot was being plowed and the police would get in at six am. Customers will most likely be waiting at the door hungry for Black Friday Door Busters and up to 80% off in the auditorium. The thought of Crazy Prices,

Chapter 11: The Piper Is Calling

Davey's scream and subsequent thump at the bottom of the escalator jarred everyone awake. This time Clyde didn't hurry. He knew it was another death. There was no reason to try to catch the killer. Clyde knew that he already got away. The question was who bit the dust, bought the farm, ate the whole enchilada, this time? As he walked around the bottom of the escalator, he saw Davey's twisted form. Clyde leaned down. Davey was trying to say something. With his dying breath, he gasped out, "Who's the man?" Then he drifted off to the other side, that great Men's Department in the sky.

Clyde looked up at Frank who had slowly

make sure no one made a mistake. He straightened the racks and finally decided it was time to call it quits. As he walked away, Davey called back to Eric's splayed body, "Who's the man, Eric?" He cupped his ear and waited for Eric's answer. "That's right. Davey's the MAN! DAVEY IS THE MAN!"

He got to the bottom of the escalator and began to rise on the moving steps. Davey examined his reflection in the plexiglas on the way up. He was certainly the man. Davey pointed at the reflection and said, "You are the man, now, Davey." He wasn't watching ahead of him until it was too late. He never noticed the ominous figure that stood atop of the escalator.

It was too late when two strong hands grabbed him and threw him back down the escalator as the killer said, "I am the man, Woody."

we should be in good shape as long as we put everyone here to work until we close Black Friday night."

"They will do it for the sake of the store, for the sake of Mr. B," said Val.

Throughout the furniture gallery, tired co-workers were snoring and whispering. All they wanted to do was get home and be safe. They were thankful that they had made it this far. By this time, they all believed that although Kellie may have canceled the Twelve Days of Christmas game--the killer hadn't. Only three lines from the song were left. No one wanted to be one of the three remaining victims on Michael's game card.

Davey, aka Woody, was confident that he would replace Eric as the manager, so confident that he sneaked to the first floor department and was checking over the stock. He had to step over Eric several times to get to his destination. Davey spoke to the stiffening cadaver as he merrily danced around him swinging his arms in the air while twisting and leaping.

"This wasn't the way I wanted to move up in this store, Eric. You were always a good friend and I always thought you would get an Assistant Manager position somewhere. But, I AM THE MAN, now, Eric. Who's the man, Eric? Who's the man now, Eric?" Davey cupped his ear close to Eric's blue, dead lips. "Davey, he's the man! What was that Eric? Did you say, Davey is the man now?" Davey twerked like Miley from fixture to fixture saying, "Who's the man, now Eric?"

He finished checking all the sign toppers to

to the others in furniture.

Kirk had once again exited his office and was relaying the good news that the County Prison would work release another twenty-five prisoners to work the store. Pat was thrilled that they would make it through the Christmas season. Val brought up the tough question of who would manage each department.

"Some of the departments, like Misses, have only one or two left. I always said that if I could get rid of this set of managers I would bring in the ones from Beaver. Butler has good managers, or rather had good managers, Eric excluded, but Beaver's managers all have a soft spot in my heart. We'll make it though the night, the season and the following year. After that, I am retiring. I don't think any manager of a store has survived after a serial killer was loose in their store," Pat stated. She knew this would be the end of her career. She sighed in exasperation before finally saying what she was truly thinking, "Why couldn't this have happened to Beaver. They deserve it not us."

"I almost forgot," said Kirk. "The state police called. The snow storm has stopped and they have already started digging us out. They expect to get to our doors in about two hours. That means we could have customers by six am. That is good news. We have to make sure they take the bodies off the floor first and use the employee's entrance. I've called all the workers who were not scheduled and told them to come in as soon as they can. Stacy can handle that side of the store. We didn't lose anyone in Juniors. Once the dead weight, er I mean, corpses are gone,

Chapter 10: Oh Lord, He's Leaping

Tired and scared, the co-workers went back to the couches and La-Z-Boys to rest and sleep. Pat and Val stood guard as Frank and Clyde checked the store once again. Their first stop was the cash office. Judy, Kaylee, Teresa and Shawna had locked themselves in and were relatively safe. Elaine had chosen to guard the Lottery Scratch-off machine. When they came upon her, she had over one hundred tickets in front her, scratching away at all of them. Next they checked the walkway from the entrance back through sweepers, into toys, then onto children's and finally furniture. It was safe. No one lurked. They came back to track even chipmunks through dense wooded hills. This trail of blood on the floor should lead us right to the killer. Follow me," Clyde said as he pointed down to the red drops on the floor. Kellermeyer was going to have a difficult day getting the store ready for customers.

They followed the red drops on the floor to the swinging doors. They went through and it led directly to the break room. Using his stealth moves Clyde motioned to Frank to stay quiet. He pointed two fingers to his eyes and one to the door, then leaped to the other side of the doorway. Then Clyde counted with his fingers, 3-2-1. The two burst in, with their Nerf guns drawn, to see the Candyman standing there eating his meatball sub lathered with red sauce. With each bite, a bit of the sauce dripped to the floor. It wasn't a blood trail they were following but marinara sauce from Tony's lunch packed by his sweet and loving mother, for only a mother could love the Candyman.

got at the Doorbuster in the Shoe Department, and slicing the killer's hand as he wrapped it around the door, we never would have escaped. Lana is our hero," said Brooke with adoring and well shadowed eyes in three shades of gray.

"That was a close one. That should be a lesson, that we must all stick together. We walk together and we move together. No one can be left behind," Pat said again.

"Does that one still count on the game card, even though no one died?" Michael asked. He was scratching it off as he asked. Loyal, Kenny and Trout from the dock scratched off theirs as well. "Ten Lords a Leaping is the next item on the list. Does anyone have that one yet?"

"Michael, if you don't stop that then you will be next, only I will do the murder," Mark stated.

"Don't be pissed just because I'm ahead of you in the game," Michael snapped back as Mark scratched off the next one on his game card.

At that point, Frank turned to Mark and said, "I don't think anyone will stop you." The others laughed and the air lightened. While most people were laughing Frank walked over to Clyde and whispered, "Kellie is no longer a suspect and from what they said, it sounds like it is a man. Any ideas?"

"Don't be fooled by a pretty face, Frank. I wouldn't count that woman out yet. She has that dangerous look in her eyes. Instead let's concentrate on these blood drops. Before the military, I was an Indian tracker and a Royal Canadian Mountie. I was raised in a log cabin that I helped my Dad build in Western Canada. It was rough territory but I learned

Only Rich and Tim are off from our department. Rich would never travel in this weather. That leaves him out. However, Tim is a possibility," Cheryl told Sean.

"That guy is a little weird. I see the way he leers at you when you're not looking. Then he starts slobbering on himself," Sean said.

"It couldn't be him, though. He hates the stairs. Besides he's too old to go running through the halls, he glows in the dark, and he tends to wander too much. I have a feeling he'll get his some time, some place but not now. It has to be someone else. Who haven't we seen that is working tonight?" she asked.

"Judy is on but I haven't seen her all night. She has that sinister look to her. That kid, Justin, is one I haven't trusted since he got here. He has a dark, swarthy look. And if you remember, we haven't seen Janine since the Accessories Department was attacked. Right now, my money is on Janine. If we find her then we may find the killer. Let's go find out what happened to the Cosmetics girls," he said. Cheryl and Sean left the storeroom and walked across the store to the bathrooms.

Instead of seeing sad, deflated co-workers, the two came upon a joyous group. Brooke was standing in front of everyone telling the story.

"As everyone knows, it takes a lot longer for us girls to use the restroom and fix our make-up. Kellie opened the door to lead us out and saw a dark figure ready to enter with a large knife. She tried to push the door shut on the killer but that person was strong. If it wasn't for Lana pulling a switchblade from her over the knee, black leather boots, that she decided to trust him and walked towards the door.

"Listen, Cheryl, when I was laying on the mattress back in the corner, I heard footsteps in your storage area. As I opened the door, another door shut. I wasn't sure which one but I guessed and made the right choice. I saw someone sliding down the center rail on the back stairs. There is someone else in the store. The killer isn't one of us," Sean told her convincingly.

"Sean, you could be telling me all this just so I no longer suspect you. Why should I believe you?" Cheryl told him as she folded her arms across her ample chest. She wanted to believe him but there was enough doubt in her mind to hold his story in dubious question. "Did you recognize this alleged other person that you saw sliding down the steps?"

"No, but this isn't the first time I nearly caught him. I was on his tail when Eric was stabbed. It wasn't a big loss with Eric, but still I almost had the killer. I saw the ring case broken into as I was paying my respects to Adam and grabbing a few carrots. It hadn't been that way earlier so I knew it was a recent event. I listened for a sound and thought I heard a moan coming from Young Mens. That was when I saw Davey come running down the escalator with Marlene right behind him. By the time I caught up to Davey, he was kneeling over Eric and the killer disappeared," Sean explained. "Whoever the killer is, he knows every back way through the store. It has to be someone who has been here for awhile, who knows the secret places and has access to them and someone we would never suspect."

"Or someone who wasn't scheduled to work.

Chapter 9: Nine Ladies Dancing

As soon as it was announced about the missing Cosmetics Department, Cheryl looked for Sean. She was still convinced he was the killer. Once again, he was nowhere to be seen. Then she heard the door at the back of furniture, that headed into the housewares storeroom and down the back staircase, open. There he stood. He motioned for Cheryl to come to him quietly. She didn't want to go. She thought he was luring her to an out of the way place in order to bring her to an early grave. At the same time, Sean had always been her friend. Cheryl the stack of bodies in the shoe department.

Frank knew he had to be strong for the whole team. He approached the last two stiff figures posed as mannequins. "These two are Lindsey and Barb," Frank said with tears in his eyes before putting on his big boy panties and then said to the others "Alright, everyone back to the Furniture Department. Let's go."

Once they got there, Val took another head count. She reported that the entire Cosmetics Department was missing. No one had seen them exit the Ladies Room. Clyde headed back to escort them to safety.

wrapping."

"No need," Melissa said, "I can tell it is Pete. See his pointer finger is missing a part of it. It is Pete for sure. Why would anyone kill Pete? That is pointless."

"Pointless, I get it," said Kaylee and she broke into laughter.

"Get what?" said Melissa.

"He's missing his pointer finger. He's pointless," Kaylee said as she laughed harder.

"If one of the mannequins is a co-worker then we better check behind the sunglasses and hats of the others," Frank instructed.

"This one is Linda," Val said. Everyone gasped as she pulled the hat off the second one and revealed Jackie. "It's Jackie. She looks so good. Her make-up is so perfectly done. Like it was professionally applied." All the eyes glanced from one cosmetic worker to another.

"Wait a second," Katie responded. "I am strictly fragrances. The rest of them are the make-up people especially Brooke." Brooke took two steps her way with her fists clenched. Heather stepped in between them. Nobody messed with Heather.

Clyde had moved to the last of the mannequins and removed their disguises. "It's Amy and Becky from jewelry." Joyce and Sue walked up to them. Joyce turned to Sue and said, "They look so peaceful. Look at that angelic smile on Amy. I always thought she was such a beautiful girl."

"That ought to up my commissions for the year," Sue remarked. At the sound of the word commissions everyone heard Rich moan loudly from

Courtesy Counter. It had to be the ugliest mannequin she ever saw.

"Kaylee, Shawna, Hannah, Ashley look at the one over there. That broad has a too much facial hair to fit in," Elaine said. Teresa stared and stared at the dummy then grabbed Shawna and Kaylee and pulled them around the counter for a closer look.

Frank and Clyde studied the other seven mannequins standing still with milk cartons taped to their hands. Michael walked up behind them and said, "Eight maids a milking. That's another one scratched off the game card." He glanced over his shoulder at Kellie and said, "What was it that I win once I get all twelve?"

Kellie pushed by him without answering, heading into the bathroom. As she did so, Frank and Clyde heard a stifled scream and snapped their heads towards the Courtesy Counter. Teresa screamed and Kaylee uttered an expletive as naturally as one drinks a glass of water. It wasn't a mannequin but a co-worker wearing a summer beach hat and sunglasses.

"Who is it, Kaylee?" Frank asked.

"Hey, if you think I'm touching a dead body to find out then you have another think coming, buddy. Kaylee doesn't do dead bodies," she uttered without an expletive.

"Neither does Shawna," Shawna added.

"You can count Teresa out, too," said Teresa. Ashley and Hannah took three steps back to avoid being asked.

"Get out of the way, I'll do it," grumped Elaine as she pushed by them. "I've handled lots of dead bodies after they waited too long in line for gift am on the clock in the Gifts Department (also on sale for $79.99), Frank announced it was time for everyone to hit the bathrooms together.

The remaining co-workers stood and stretched. One yawn led to another but they were all glad to stand and move. As they trudged towards the restrooms, Kirk walked up next to Frank, Val and Pat. "I just got off the phone with the Warden at the County Prison. He says he can give us twenty-five men and women on a work release but they will have to wear their orange jumpsuits while working," he told them.

"Orange at Christmas? That is preposterous!" Val chortled.

"Orange is the new black, Val," responded Pat. "Are they giving us armed guards as well?"

"These are their best prisoners. I don't think we'll need them for these prisoners," answered Kirk.

"Not for the prisoners but to keep our own people in line," Pat snapped. Frank agreed.

As the group passed the check-out area in Housewares, close to the As Seen On TV section filled with items you can't live without, they saw eight figures standing in front of the doors to the restroom in a straight line that hid the amazing collection of decorative art at the crazy price of 50% off. Kaylee turned to Shawna, who had returned for Christmas help, and said, "That scared me but who in the world would put mannequins over here."

"My heart leaped in my mouth. That is spooky," Shawna answered. Elaine had stopped at the lottery scratch-offs to play a few dollars before turning around to see the mannequin behind the

Chapter 8: Eight Mannequins a Milk Drinking

The next hour passed slowly as most of those that were left, sat tired and scared. No one moved without someone else watching their twist or turn with a large degree of suspicion. A few had managed to slip away for extracurricular activity. They knew because Vicki's lab coat was hung across a kitchen chair, on sale for only $79.99. As the chimes hit four

He pulled his walkie-talkie out and depressed the button.

"Frank, you better come down to Petites. We lost six more valuable co-workers. And you better alert Ed from Kellermeyer that there is a lot of clean-up to be done before we open tomorrow," he stated.

The remaining co-workers raced with Frank down the escalator. Except for Kirk, he had to go back to the computer to change his posting on Craigslist. He needed six more workers.

Michael looked at his game card. There were seven at that scene. He scratched off Seven Swans a Swimming.

collection. Gretchen had slipped through Cosmetics and grabbed some eyeshadows. With three fingers dipped into the pods of color she drew three stripes from her eyes to her jawbone. Gretchen was going to war and her warpaint, in various non-allergenic colors, from the Claris collection, would tell the killer she was serious about avenging her sister. Donna pulled her bandanna from her purse that she used when riding the motorcycle while Debbie Green and Marie hid in the two dressing rooms. They were loaded to bare and ready to kill. Sharon climbed to the top of the Petite's dressing room and waiting like a panther to attack her prey. With the six hidden, all that was left was for Stacy to put in her earphones and bop around the department. Stacy danced, gyrating her body to each tune, dreaming of Johnny Depp. If her lithe, sexy form didn't attract a killer then nothing else would.

Twenty minutes went by and no killer had approached Stacy. Suddenly she felt a hand grip her shoulder. She had no fear, for she knew her six co-workers, in touch with their inner-bitches, would be charging at the villain anytime. She wheeled around to see who the killer was. She looked into the eyes of Clyde who was talking to her. She couldn't hear him with her ear buds blaring. He pulled one out.

"Why are you down here by yourself?" he asked.

"I'm not. There are six armed women with Nerf guns watching my every move," she stated knowing at any moment Clyde would be pummeled by Nerf bullets. Clyde looked around. He started to count the six pools of blood in a circle around Stacy.

need a hunk of bait that will draw attention. Someone who will talk a lot, even to herself," Connie stated.

"How about that new girl, Tori, in your department, Kim?" asked Gretchen.

"No, she is too good to lose," Kim answered.

"And I am expendable?" retorted Connie.

"You are getting a little long in the tooth, Connie," answered Kim.

"Shelley?" questioned Debbie.

"That won't work. Everyone loves Shelley. Besides if we lost her then Pat would make us all get more credit apps to make up for the loss," said Marie.

"Not everyone. Stacy would wipe her out just to be the lead credit app co-worker in the store once again," Kim stated. They all agreed that Shelley wouldn't be a good choice but possibly Stacy would be ideal. With their plan set, they pulled Stacy into their new circle of The Seven Avengers, slipped out the rear door and down the stairs. This time they would be prepared with weapons. Gretchen had gone to the toy department and grabbed Nerf guns for everyone. The guns were part of the Black Friday specials. She had opened each package carefully so she could repackage them for sale afterward. She was always thrifty and always thinking.

The plan was to have Stacy work in the Petite Department alone while the other six laid in wait, guns in hand. The six were hidden behind displays and clothes. Kim found a camouflage night shirt and pulled it over her clothing. She tied panty hose around her head, ala Rambo, then sat in the middle of a rack of clothing waiting with a vicious snarl spread across her faintly lip-sticked lips from the Clinique

"What plan do you have? I am tired of waiting around for Kellie's little game to come to an end. I think she is responsible. We've got to take her out and do it now," Kim said in a quiet tone as she drove her left fist into her right palm with a resounding thud. Her eyes flashed with the desire to kill Kellie.

"How do you propose we eliminate her?" asked Donna.

"Personally, I want to strangle her with my bare hands," said Debbie. "Then again, that's how I'd like to deal with a bunch of our whiny, cry-baby customers, too," she added in her sweet and innocent demeanor. The shocking statement took the others by surprise.

"Or hang her with an Infinity scarf," Connie added.

"Instead of sitting here whining let's do something. We are close to the back steps to the first floor. Let's slip downstairs and set a trap. Any ideas?" Kim said. She looked right at Marie and Sharon for ideas.

"My family is famous for hunting and trapping in the area," said Debbie Green. "I learned from my grandfather to lay a trap by using bait. Who is going to be the bait? I suggest Candy. If she gets knocked off then I move up a slot at the store."

Although absolutely no one had a problem with using Candy, all eyes shifted towards Connie.

"Wait a minute. I am not the hero kind. I just want to get home and be alive when I get there. Count me out when it comes to bait. Count me out of the whole thing. I suggest you find someone who doesn't know the plan. Someone willing just to help out. We

TV show that thinks outside the box."

Bucky butted in, "Jody's a writer. She can figure it out."

"If this were a mystery novel, how would you write it, Jody?" Leah asked as she slid to the edge of the couch, leaning forward with her seductive cleavage.

"Gosh, I don't know. I guess I would try to have everyone suspect all the wrong people. It's called a misdirect. You leave just enough clues to direct people to the wrong person. That way the killer can do what they want to do while everyone else is watching the suspects. Right now it looks like Sean did it but what if the killer waited for Sean to go missing, killed his victims, then moved on. Or take Kellie. She came up with the Twelve Days of Christmas game. All you have to do is tie together clues to the song and you have Kellie as the lead suspect. How would the killer know about the game ahead of time? Kellie has the motive, the skills and the knowledge. A smart killer will misdirect like a magician's sleight of hand trick," Jody told them as Sean plopped down on the couch next to Cheryl and punched her in the arm. It was known to all that he lived up to his nickname: The Tormentinator.

Back by the mattresses sat seven women from various departments. The seven were distraught. They had all lost friends and relatives. Gretchen turned to Kim from the Misses department and said in a cold, bloodthirsty way, "I don't think Clyde, or Frank, or Pat will find the killer before the police arrive in the morning. We need to do something. I want to catch that killer and avenge my sister."

Gathered around the furniture sales desk were Dave, Leah, Garry, Cheryl, Jody and Bucky. They were talking in low voices so no one could hear them.

"I am sure it's Sean," stated Cheryl with anger in her eyes. "Remember when he tried to kill me by giving me the strawberry beer that night. I've had my suspicions ever since."

Dave, always the voice of reason and deep, reflective contemplation after a few shots, said, "Cheryl, I think you are jumping to conclusions. There are others who were missing during key moments when the murders were committed. Kellie is as likely a suspect as Sean. She is trying to climb the ladder in this food chain called the Big B. Then you have Clyde, a trained military killer. What about Frank? He can move about the store freely with no one watching. He seems to be missing at all the key moments. And Davey was found with a knife in his hand. Don't forget Janine is missing as well and not presumed to be dead. She left with the Accessories Department but wasn't found hanging with them or anywhere else. She has been a little crazy lately. I overheard her say that she had a stalker in the store that appeared mysteriously behind her at strange times then pointed two fingers to his eyes then one finger back at her. That stalker could be the killer as well. Then there is the Juniors Department. I haven't seen them all night. Melissa and Amy are pretty dangerous in their own rights. There are too many possibilities to eliminate anyone right away or to conclude that Sean did it. I agree, Sean is a little twisted in the head but he is not the only suspect. What we need is someone like that guy on the Castle

Chapter 7: Seven Workers a Whining

The co-workers once again assembled in the Furniture Department. Val pulled a list of those scheduled to work and compared to the names of those who would not be working ever again, actually those who could not work again or rather those who had met an early demise or was it a permanent termination? Clyde took it from Val and went down the list of those who remained. He checked his list to see who was naughty and who was nice. Only Vicki had been naughty. He wanted to know who was missing for those few would be his prime suspects. He was also interested in anyone who called off sick. It could be one of them.

could talk to her straight without getting a shiv stuck in his side.

"Dave will keep an eye on him for the rest of the night," Leah said. "Maybe we need to go outside for a few minutes to calm you down."

Cheryl turned around. Sean was gone again.

managers at Beaver and bring them in to replace all of you. There is no bright side. Well, maybe losing Eric could be viewed as a bright point, but everyone else is not. I suggest we all go back to furniture and no one leave. We stay together. We don't separate."

Sean was standing in the rear of the group munching on a half done carrot when Cheryl tapped him on the shoulder. "Where were you? I have been looking all over the store for you. Every time someone dies, you are nowhere to be found until afterward. Are you doing this?" she asked.

"Lighten up, Cheryl. You need to get off my back. BELIEVE me, if I was doing it, you would've been FIRST," Sean said as he bit down again on his carrot.

Cheryl stared at him. "Is that from Adam's crock pot?"

"Yeah, but they aren't done yet. Kate's are closer to being done. Her stew has a sweeter taste to it than Adam's," he told her. "Then again, Kate was a sweet girl. Adam's stew tastes like a salty, old pirate."

"How could you do that?" she asked with disgust in her voice.

"I gave a carrot to Adam, too."

Cheryl stormed away. She planned to tell Clyde that Sean was the killer. Dave and Leah were standing in her pathway, a dangerous place to be when she was on a mission.

"Cheryl, chill out. If I could send you home right now, then I would. We know what you are going to do. Don't. If you accuse Sean and it is somebody else then you will lose a good friend," Dave said. When Cheryl was in one of her moods only Dave co-worker left in the department. That isn't suspicious, is it? So, who did it, Shayne? Satan?"

"How can you say that, Jess? These were my friends," Shayne said as she broke into tears. Shayne heard a soft moan from the pile of bodies under the shoes at the sound of the word commission. It was Rich. She quickly snatched a stiletto heel and gave him a hard rap to his head.

"Shayne, I was kidding. I thought we just needed to lighten up the mood a little. A few people get murdered and everyone is so gloomy. It is the Christmas season. Why don't we sing some Christmas Carols to get us all back in the Christmas Spirit. We need to have a little more joy in our hearts. And, that is going to be one heckuva commission check this month, Shayne," she added as she winked at Shayne.

At the second sound of the word commission, Shelby moaned loudly. Shayne once again grabbed a stiletto heel and punctured her forehead.

"You're right, Jess. I do need to look on the bright side," Shayne said with a smile stretching across her face. "It CERTAINLY will be one heckuva commission check, woo-hoo! Money, money, monnn-nayyy."

At the third sound of the word commission, Sue and Neil groaned and moaned. Grabbing a matched set of thin stiletto heels, Shayne, using a rare double handed but swift move, struck them at the same time ending their death bed protestations.

"Wait a second everyone," Pat said. "Where is the bright side to all this? I've lost friends and good managers tonight. If I lose more managers then I will have to call my most cherished, greatly favored

Chapter 6: Six Shoes a Stomping

The rest of the co-workers rode the escalator down to see what had happened. As they all got off the motorized steps, Shayne charged into the mix screaming. "Come quick, it's Sue, and Dennis, and Rich, and Shelby, and Susan Rowles and Janet. They've been stomped and buried under the shoes."

The co-workers hurried to the department and the scene was exactly as Shayne described it. As Jess from coats and dresses walked up she remarked, "That's convenient, Shayne. Here we are facing Black Friday and you are the only commissioned based shoe

In case anyone wants to know, the potatoes are done. The carrots are still a little crunchy, though."

work my butt off for the few months that I am here in this desolate town of Butler. I deserve the position."

David and his son, Tyler, protested. They felt the job should go to Davey, the man known affectionately to all as Woody.

It was Kirk who finally settled it. "That will be Pat's decision. Let's not worry about that sort of thing now or about the trivial loss of Eric. In fact, that may a good thing. There is a bigger problem at hand. I have several recently vacated positions in the accessories, men's, visuals and security departments. If you know of anyone who is looking for a job, have them stop in my office after they have cleared the snow away. I can promise them instant hiring on the spot. No questions asked."

Clyde knelt down next to Eric and looked closely. On his hand were five golden rings and his steel hardened body had been punctured by five stab wounds. "Frank, I haven't seen this since Beirut, or was it Lebanon. I think we are dealing with a professional killer, potentially a crazed, insane terrorist. It reminds me of the time I took a black ops team into Czechoslovakia. This is exactly how we took out the terrorists there. Although finding five rings for each body's hand was hell. I don't like how this looks. As the new Lord of security, I want everyone to tie themselves in a chair upstairs until the police come in the morning."

As he finished, Sean walked up behind the group. "What happened here?"

"Someone has killed Eric," Frank answered. "Where were you when this happened?"

"I was hungry so I paid my respects to Adam.

Heather said as she folded her arms, displaying her colorful ink. Vicki just walked in as they were talking. She was straightening her black outfit and white lab coat but her hair was still a mess and her lipstick was smeared on her satisfied lips and smile.

"That is ridiculous," Kellie screamed back at them.

"I guess I have the first four clues, then," Michael said as he folded up the game card and placed it in his back pocket.

Kellie's defense of herself was interrupted by a scream from below them all. Clyde once again led a troop of co-workers to the escalator. Pat's heels clicked close on his heels. This was going to be a bad day. She mumbled to herself, "Do they sell wine by the barrel?"

As the group exited the bottom of the escalator, they saw Davey, aka Woody, on his knees next to the apparently expired body of the once lively and lovely Eric. Blood dripped from Woody's fingers as he held the blue, ceramic coated Santoku knife in the air. He was screaming, "No, no. Not Eric. He was my friend. Why couldn't it have been Larry?"

Eric gasped for a postmortem breath. Davey leaned down to hear his dying words, "Woody, stay away from Jackie."

As Frank laid his hand on Davey's shoulder and removed the bloody knife from the man's grip, Davey turned to him first with tears in his eyes then a sudden crazed looked of glee. "I guess that makes me the manager of the men's department, now. It is only right that the management position goes to me."

"What do you mean?" Larry screamed. "I

to return."

"While we're waiting, I have a question," stated Michael from the loading dock. "Kellie announced a game earlier. So far, I have Chad in a pear tree, two security people with turtle necks and peaceful as doves, three french hens if you count Kate and Adam and now four hanging birds. Have I missed any of the clues so far?" Michael was marking off the game card distributed earlier. Kenny and Loyal pulled their game cards from their back pockets and checked them against the evening's events.

Kellie jumped up, frustrated and exasperated. "Michael, those are not part of the game. The game is canceled. If it was part of the game then I would have to be the killer."

"Are you?" Jackie from Petites asked.

"I certainly am not. Yes, I am frustrated that I am here tonight, locked in a store and snowed in. But I did not kill them. I have been with my girls the whole time," Kellie stated adamantly. "Tell them girls."

"Not the whole time, Kellie. You left to check our stockroom earlier before the Accessories Department got wiped out," Kristle stated with a deeply dimpled smile.

"And you said you had to check your email before Adam and Kate were discovered," Katie added.

"Then there was the time you took our internet orders back just before we found Kolby and Drew," Karen stated in an accusatory manner.

"Let us not forget how you needed to check on a shipment on the dock when we first came in,"

Chapter 5: Five Bloody Stab Wounds

Clyde tried to calm everyone down. He had just walked the perimeter of the store's second floor. He reported that there was no one hiding anywhere. He continued, "Eric and Mark have done the same thing on the first floor. They should be back upstairs in a few minutes. I believe whoever the killer is, they have escaped the store. Unless someone is missing or was missing during the murders, we have to assume they are gone. Let's relax and wait for Mark and Eric one with a scarf with white birds covering the red faux silk. After his initial shock he walked on thinking that the buyers would have to put those scarves on sale soon. He wondered how much mark-up he could add to them after he bought them on sale and re-sold them at his store downtown. When he walked into the break room, Sean was standing at the soda machine waiting for his bottle of Dew to drop.

"Sean, I am having a snack now, could you let Frank know there are four co-workers from Accessories hanging in the hallway," the Candyman said. As he said it, Cheryl walked in the breakroom cursing Sean.

"You told me you were going to the men's room and that was fifteen minutes ago. I waited for you and you never came out. What have you been doing all this time?"

"Getting some peace and quiet from your nagging and a plastic bottle of pop," he said. "By the way, Candyman said there are four women hanging in the hallway. The only one missing from the group is Janine. You better let Frank know," Sean told her. Sean sat down to sip his Dew as the Candyman started heating his snack for his break. Cheryl raced to the furniture department.

more cranky." There was still no answer from Janine. "Do I have to come down there, Janine?" Still no answer.

Tori stomped down the steps. She punched the stop button as she hit the bottom. She looked around. She walked down to the break room and stared inside. No Janine. By this point, Tori was furious and raced back to the steps to the third floor. "Terri, Shayna and Jackie, come down and help me find Janine." There was no answer from the storage area. "Quit playing games, girls." Tori stomped up the steps.

Back at furniture, the Candyman stood up. He told Faithanne, Emily and Susanna that he was going back to eat his lunch. His dear, loving mother had given him a large piece of lasagna, a Caesar salad, a foot long hoagie filled with homemade meatballs smothered in a basil based marinara sauce, a pound of carved turkey, stuffing, mashed potatoes and sweet potato pie for his break meal and another completely filled cooler for his lunch. Faithanne was fearful for Tony but Susanna told him to go ahead but leave his key because she wasn't going to go through the pockets of dead man just to find his key as she waved her hand in a dismissive way.

"Who would want to harm the Caaandymaaan? I make everything satisfying and delicious. You can even eat my dishes. Everyone loves the Caaandymaaan," he continued down the hall past the offices. As he turned the corner to head to the break room, he saw it. There were four sets of feet dangling. The four girls had been hung by festive, Christmas scarves. One with an Infinity scarf, one with an Eternity scarf, one with a Figure 8 scarf and from soap to nuts, crayons to casseroles, pots to zebras. They overheard Melissa telling Pete he couldn't count the items since he only had 9 ½ fingers. The girls walked past Val and Pat sitting in the main office fretting about the extra hours they would have to use to make up for the store closing. Shayna broke down again as they walked by the security office. Their biggest shock came as they strolled by the training room. There was Marlene chasing Davey around the training table. Janine scoffed out, "Kids nowadays."

Once in the back, the five headed up one more flight of steps to their fully stocked storage area. They began pulling boxes and setting them on the conveyor belt. Janine went to the bottom of the belt and began unloading onto an empty flatbed cart while the others continued sending boxes down the belt.

After the boxes were flowing quickly and easily, Terri noticed that Janine was allowing the boxes to crash on the floor. "Tori, Janine must need help. The boxes are piling up at the bottom of the conveyor belt."

"Janine, what is wrong with you? Can't you keep up?" Tori scolded then laughed because Janine was the hardest worker and most conscientious person in the store (in Janine's mind only). Although, she often needed watching by her stalker. This night, though, her stalker had called off sick. No one answered. "Janine, don't play games. This is not the time for games. I don't like games. You know, I do not have a sense of humor, Janine." The other workers shook their heads in agreement. "I need more coffee therefore, I am cranky and you are making me cantankerous, Adam seemed to stay to himself, locked away in the Housewares stockroom, known as Adam's Lair, alone and mysterious.

Garry and Leah sat away from the others discussing the fact that only Sean had been missing for a long period of time. When Jody joined them, they hushed but she brought the topic up. "I think it is Sean," she said matter of factly.

"We all know Sean. He may be psycho but not that psycho. In fact, he and Adam were friends," Leah responded.

"He has been a little off lately, though," Garry tossed in. "Remember the other day when he throttled that little old lady that wasted an hour of his time. I had to pull him off her. She went running out of the store and fortunately she has never come back."

"Okay," said Leah. "I guess we need to keep a better eye on him but personally I am not going to be the one to do it."

The discussion among the girls from the Accessories Department was different. Tori, Janine, Jackie and Terri were all trying to console Shayna, who had just lost her brother, Kolby. She was weeping and rocking back and forth (more for show). It was Tori who came up with the idea to work in the stock room to get their minds of it. Terri thought better of it but when Janine and Tori lifted Shayna from a lovely, black leather recliner with vibrating massage cushions and a tilt back, on sale for only $799.99, she joined in with her co-workers.

The five walked back along the hall past the Auditorium, where Pete, Melissa, southern belle Tiffany and Waylon were unpacking boxes of items

Chapter 4: Four Hanging Birds

Frank made the announcement to the group of co-workers still crashed on the furniture in the second floor department. Most took it pretty hard. The jewelry department girls took it the hardest with the loss of Kate. She was always sweet and generous with the attention and care for others. Whereas, Adam was a person that not many knew. Although never

Sean? You're eating Adam's finger."

"It's only a carrot, Cheryl. I'm hungry and I like carrots. See, he held out the uneaten portion of the carrot to show her.

"You know, Sean, you were the only person unaccounted for when these five people were killed. Where were you?" she asked with more suspicion than ever.

"I was where I am going now. I need a smoke. Are you coming?" Sean asked.

was cooking it?"

David lifted the lid of the next pot. Staring back at him was the grinning face of his old friend, Adam. Adam's head was floating in a well seasoned, tomato based stew accompanied by potatoes, carrots and fingers. Dave dropped the lid to the floor and it broke into pieces. His face was ashen as he told the others, "It is Adam," he gasped as he buried his face in his hands. "He deserved better than this. He deserved something better than a purple, 19.99 Bella Dot Non-programmable Slow Cooker. He hated purple. He, at least, deserved a Hamilton-Beach top of the line, Stay and Go cooker. We can look on the bright side, though, the killer used a slow cooker liner, on sale for $1.99 in the Small Appliances department. It will make it easier for the forensics team for clean-up."

"That is a good point, Dave," Frank said. "We can still sell the crock pots but I'd give a 20% discount."

Eric raised the other lid. "It is Kate," he said.

Joyce moved over to look. "She looks so peaceful and natural," she said. Her co-worker from the Jewelry Department, Sue, looked in at Kate.

"She looks over cooked to me," Sue retorted.

Amy sauntered over in her provocative way and peered inside. "I always liked those earrings. Do you think she still needs them?"

Sean moved towards the crock. Cheryl stayed by his side. They stared in at the Adam stew. Sean reached into the pot and plucked up an item. He placed it in his mouth and bit down.

Cheryl screamed at him, "What are you doing,

workers right behind him.

"That's like sending the spider after the fly," Dan said as he straightened his curtains.

"What kind of comment was that?" Mary Ellen fired at Dan.

"With Kolby and Drew out of the way, Clyde would be head of security. If you ask me, those murders were his ticket to the top with a big, fat salary increase and the coveted title of Head of Security. Men have died for less," Dan said. "Come to think of it, Mary Ellen, your demise would put me in line to manage the Gifts Department. Don't you have to check the stockroom for something?"

"That's ridiculous, Dan. You don't know it but Clyde is a former CIA, NSA and FBI agent," Mary Ellen said.

"A government trained killer," Chase the Playa' added, "I feel better already. Maybe Dan is right."

Nancy looked at the others. She shook her head. "I was sitting next to Clyde on the couch. He was nowhere near the killings. If he is truly a government agent then I feel safer that the store is in his hands."

Clyde's entourage, going down the escalator, consisted of the Housewares department, Sean, Joyce and the Men's clothing department. It was a group big enough to protect each other. Following their noses, the group made it to the jewelry department. All along the watch counter sat three crock pots, cooking well-seasoned stews. Clyde approached slowly and lifted the first lid and turned to the others, "It is a cornish French hen," he said with relief. "But who

"Chad in a pear tree and two turtle necked security people. This is starting to freak me out," said Leah. David put his arm around her as a display of heroic strength and then she asked a question that would cause them all to wonder, "What's the next part of the song? Three french hens?"

The entire store gathered in the furniture department. Pat broke the sad news of the three murders and Frank went over the strategy for the night. "As Pat said, the police cannot possibly get in here until the morning. Both the freight elevator and security office are secured. We cannot violate the crime scenes. Once the cops get here then they will need to question everyone. In the meantime, we need to get our minds off these gruesome murders. Everyone needs to go back to their departments but keep on eye on each other. Don't even go to the bathroom alone. Clyde will circulate through the store and question you. Now, let's do an inventory. Are all your department members present?"

Everyone looked around and counted. Dave spoke up, "Adam is missing." Joyce, the jewelry department manager added that Kate was also missing.

"They are walking through the mall but should be waiting by the front door," Pat informed everyone.

Justin, who was standing closest to the escalator, broke the silence with an unusual statement. "I smell something cooking downstairs. Are we having food in every department?" That was all Clyde needed to hear, he hurried toward the escalator with Frank at his heels and several brave co-

Chad was a great guy and good friend but who in the world listened to that old funk music anyway," Sean said as he walked away.

"Then you admit you killed him?" Mark asked as he stepped forward with his fists clenched.

"No, I just don't like anybody," Sean said as he left. No one wanted to say it, but they all thought it, Sean had killed Chad and now they had to spend the night in a department store alone with the killer.

"I don't think it was Sean but for the rest of the night, we need to keep an eye on him. Kolby can do that with the monitors. Wherever Sean goes then three of us need to go with him. Agreed?" Dave asked.

A moment later they heard Kim scream from down the hall. The five raced towards her. She was shaking her arms in the air wildly and screaming, "It's Kolby and Drew. They're dead!"

The six pushed the door open slowly as Clyde, Frank and Pat approached from the other end. Pat called to them, "You about scared us to death. What's all the screaming about?" She looked inside the security office and there sat Drew and Kolby in the office chairs. Their heads had been pressed in to look like turtles pulled back into their shells. Pat muttered and ran to her office to call the police. Clyde moved everyone back to secure the area then pulled the door shut.

"Frank, I think we need to call a store meeting, right away," Clyde said.

"Before you do that, you need to see the freight elevator. Chad's head is on a pear tree," Mark reported.

Claus figures and prepared to protect the women. Cheryl had already pulled a switchblade from her back pocket. She was from New Castle and never left home without it. It was a special gift given to her on her third birthday along with matches and accelerant used in burning down houses in the city. It was common in that town and most kids were experts by twelve years old.

As the steps approached, a figure appeared in the hall. It was Sean. They hadn't seen him for the last half hour. "Where were you?" Leah queried.

"I went out to have a smoke and decided to try to dig my way to the truck. I have a six pack in there and didn't want it to freeze and explode," he reported.

"Where's the six pack, bucko," said Cheryl. He was the only one unaccounted for during the time that Chad had been murdered. She always knew he was a little psycho, or he wouldn't have been such a good friend, but he was the only one unaccounted for in the last half hour.

"I didn't get very far. It is colder than I expected. So, I had another cigarette and came back in. What's wrong? You look like you saw a dead body or something," Sean joked.

Mark gestured towards the freight elevator. Sean walked over and stared inside. He took a deep breath. "Is he dead?"

"What do you think, Sean? His head is here and his body is somewhere else. I have a sneaking suspicion that he is dead," quipped Cheryl. She didn't want to think it but in her mind, Sean was suspect Numero Uno.

"Don't get your panties in a bunch, Cheryl.

Chapter 3: Three French Hens in Slow Cookers With 50% Off Sign Toppers

As Kim headed to find the security team, Cheryl, Leah, Dave, Paul and Mark, who had finally finished throwing up, waited for their return. They heard the swinging doors open and steps in the hallway. Dave and Paul picked up large, plastic Santa

No one was there. The killer had moved into the monitor room and waited for the opportunity to deliver his final blow. "Kolby was a much better fight, Drew," the killer said.

"That's because he was a god amongst mere mortals," Drew answered. "Whoever you are, you are about to face someone who has lethal fists, licensed by the state of Pennsylvania. I will destroy you," Drew spat back at his potential killer.

But without warning, the heavy sledge hammer came hurtling through the air striking him directly in the chest. Most normal men would have gone down in tears at the sheer force of the blow. Drew, though, was no normal man. He staggered back a mere six inches before his eyes flashed a glowing red. "Now, you've made me mad!" Drew exclaimed. He took two giant steps towards Kolby's killer when, without warning, and with no flash in the dim light, because it was ceramic coated Santoku knife, the blade found Drew's heart. As he fell, Drew exclaimed, "See you in hell, mother......"

knees and then to the floor. He uttered his last words, "There goes my accident free record."

The killer turned off the lights in the two rooms. The glow from the security monitors was enough light to do what the villain needed to do next. The killer pulled the amazingly well toned but now dead body of Kolby into a monitor chair. With the body positioned correctly, the killer raised a large sledge hammer over his head and prepared to bring it down pushing the skull into the neck, like a turtle receding into its shell, when a key was inserted in the lock. The killer whispered, "That must be your buddy, Drew. I'm going to really, really enjoy this."

Drew pushed open the heavy door. He saw the lights were out and reached for the switch. Before his hand got there a sledge hammer crashed into the wall next to his fingers. He leaped, leaving the locked door to glide shut, locking out any aid or help. Drew dropped to the ground and slid across the floor on Kolby's puddled blood, to the desk. The hammer came down on top of the desk. Then he heard the maniacal voice say, "You don't want to play along, Drew? We're playing the Twelve Days of Murder and right now I need two turtle doves. Kolby is one and you are two. Come out and play, Drew." The killer laughed but Drew didn't. It wasn't that Drew had no sense of humor, it was simply that he was preoccupied with his near death experiences.

Drew didn't wait for more conversation, remembering his Security Guard On-line course, he flung the desk up and in the direction of the voice, then leaped to his feet in a kung-fu pose and waited for the desk to fall to the floor and reveal his attacker.

he trained several of the store's best workers, like Connie, Justin and that quite, timid, mousey Tim, only to lose them to other departments. One couldn't say that Pete was bitter about his losses, but his recent ramblings over the store speakers about products for sale up to 80% off in the Auditorium always ended with "Or you can buy things from those traitors Tim, Justin and Connie."

The knife, that was aimed at his heart, was deflected but sliced through his arm. Kolby moved with a flash of agility, more like a caged cougar than a human being, and leaped to the side as the next cut from the knife swung his way. He yelled for Drew but the attacker was quick. The first cut, which is always the deepest according to the song that played over and over again on the PA system, left blood soaking into his shirt. Kolby knew the cut had hit an artery. The blood loss was weakening his completely muscled and hard-toned, athletic, Adonis-like frame. He tried another cat like move to deflect the swipe from the ceramic coated Santoku knife, a doorbuster item from the Auditorium, but his shoe slipped on the puddle of blood forming around his feet. This time, even after Kolby's valiant attempt to stop the killer, the knife found it's mark. Kolby backed against the wall with the knife sticking out of his chest, stared hard at the killer and said, "Is that all you got? It will take more than a blue, ceramic coated Santoku knife by Colorsplash to take me down. And by the way, where is your receipt for this item?" Kolby leaped forward and with the strength of a bear, gripped the killer. It was more than his wounded body could endure. He expired like an old box of K-cups, slipping to his and linens.

Drew flipped the switch in the training room. It seemed fine but the lights still flickered. He climbed on the table to tap the lights. None seemed to be loose. "It's the storm," he said to himself. "Most likely the whole store will go dark before the night is over. I could be home in a nice warm bed watching Scooby Doo reruns but here I am standing on a table checking lights. Not a pilfering thief to catch. Not a thing to do but climb on tables in an empty store." Drew moaned. He got back down and decided to check on the other back rooms then go over the plans for the evening with Kolby.

When Drew walked into the internet sales room, he thought he heard a yell. From his vantage point, it was hard to tell where it came from. Was it the freight elevator? Was it down the hall towards the offices? Was it one of the co-workers back in furniture? He couldn't tell but Kolby would be watching it all from the monitors. Kolby's razor sharp, eagle eye missed nothing, he thought.

At the same time Kolby entered the Security office, he slowly turned around. A blast of light hit his eyes. He threw his hand up to deflect the light but it was too late. He saw the flash of a blade. It was a blue, ceramic coated, Santoku knife from the Colorsplash Collection, on sale that day in the Auditorium for the crazy price of $1.99. Pete had been raving about them in the morning meetings. They were so good he had cut off the tip of his pointing finger with it. Pete claimed that it cut so fast and so cleanly that he didn't feel a thing. That was Pete, always looking on the bright side, even though

Chapter 2: Two Turtle Necks

Kolby, the head of security, and Drew strolled back to their security office to make sure the store was secure and that the storm had not effected any of their surveillance equipment. The lights were flickering in the training room, which was not a usual thing. Kolby instructed his partner to see what the problem was and then join him. He unlocked his door and stepped inside, pulling the door shut and locking it. Security and safety were his two primary goals. He took them as seriously as Gretchen did dust on her clothes racks and Susanna did properly folded towels

to go out as well. This is going to be one long, long night. At least we're getting paid to ride out the storm," she remarked as she got closer. The four of them had just pushed open the door to head down the stairway when they heard Paul scream out, "Oh, shit!" They turned and banged through the swinging doors to the store rooms and the freight elevator. They saw Mark bending over, heaving his Thanksgiving dinner on the floor. He was wishing he hadn't had that extra spoonful of cranberry sauce or was it blood? Had he, too, been murdered and didn't know it? Paul was frozen in place. He turned his head slowly and looked at the others.

"Don't come any closer. You don't want to see this. It is pretty bad," Paul commanded.

Telling Cheryl not to do something was like throwing gasoline on a fire. She moved forward quickly, pushed Paul out of the way, took one look and screamed. Before them all, in the freight elevator, was the Visual Department Manager, Chad, or at least part of him and not his best part according to fellow workers and girlfriends. He had been beheaded and his wide-eyed head topped a tree with plastic pears hanging from the limbs. The bloody, dripping head still had Chad's sport cap pulled tightly down over the crown. Chad's face was a hideous sight and now even more since it no longer was attached to his body but sat like a Christmas Angel atop a joyfully decorated tree. Cheryl looked at the others and choked out, through tears and the rising innards of her stomach, "Go get Kolby but don't tell anyone what's here." Kim was moving double speed back to the furniture department to find the head of security.

once the store re-opened, it would be ready to make up for lost time.

Val and Pat had prepared snacks and brought in drinks for the next day, and had left them on the loading dock, but at this point, it seemed pointless to wait. Pat looked at Mark from the dock and said, "Mark, could you and Paul bring up the food that is down on the dock. Val, Frank and I are going to get it ready so we all have something to eat."

"Did you bring wine, too, Pat?" Cheryl joked.

"It would be gone by now if I had," she retorted. "This storm is one of those 'forget the glass, give me the bottle' sort of experiences." Most people laughed and Cheryl looked around to see if Sean was nearby. She wanted to slip outside for a smoke. She didn't see him. She stood and looked across to the mattresses. He wasn't lying on his favorite one either. She turned to Leah, who sat next to her, and motioned with her head that it was time to go outside for a few minutes. Leah grabbed Dave's arm and pulled him to his feet. The three walked to the back staircase along with Mark and Paul. Paul was pushing an empty flat bed cart. No one would have recognized him with a full one.

"I wonder how my dog is doing? I expect he'll have the house torn up by the time I get home. Not much I can do about it. That puppy is something else. Did I ever show you his picture?" Paul said as he pushed the button to bring the freight elevator to the second floor. The old freight elevator groaned and shook as it rose to the second floor.

Kim, being her normal speed-walking self, had caught up to Cheryl, Leah and Dave. "I am ready collectible car stories and swapping jokes. It would be a long night for everyone especially for those listening to Garry's stories.

Adam and his girlfriend, Kate, had convinced Drew to open the mall doors so they could walk around, knowing Adam, he meant fool around. Pat wanted him to check to see if the wine store, by some unbelievable chance, was open. She did have her priorities and wine was one of them. By the time Drew had returned from letting them out, and setting a time for them to meet and get back in, he found that most of the employees had drifted towards the furniture department. Frank, the Assistant Manager, was talking to the group as Drew dropped into a La-Z-Boy chair.

"As you all know, we are stuck here. Let's try to make the best of the time. As I have always said, 'Stack 'em high and watch 'em fly.' Why don't we spend some time stocking the shelves to their fullest potential. Eventually, this storm will end and shoppers will begin their seasonal ritual."

Most of the co-workers moaned but they all knew he was right. It had been a busy week already. Mary Ellen was already complaining about dwindling stock on her shelves. She rounded up Dan, Nancy, Betty, Kamarki, Justin and Chase and charged towards her stockroom. Which was amazing since her crew charged nowhere fast. If it wasn't for the consistent hard and speedy work of Chase, President of the Playa's Club, not much got done in the department. Kim, Eric, Sue, Jackie, Jeff and Tori were co-ordinating their teams as they headed towards the escalator. It would be a long night but keep everyone happy and excited about working. Pat, the store manager and Val, the store trainer, had made food for everyone and planned to serve a midnight brunch. Kellie, an assistant manager and head of the cosmetics department had invented a game for each of the co-workers to play. She had based it on the song, *The Twelve Days of Christmas*. Each time a co-worker scratched off a block of the game they received a token. The first one with twelve tokens won a gift card. At this very expensive time of the year, gift cards always came in handy. There was only one trouble for many of the workers. No one could remember the twelve items in the song. Eventually, it was all one could hear as they walked the store.

> On the twelfth day of Christmas my true love sent to me:
> 12 Drummers Drumming
> Eleven Pipers Piping
> Ten Lords a Leaping
> Nine Ladies Dancing
> Eight Maids a Milking
> Seven Swans a Swimming
> Six Geese a Laying
> Five Golden Rings
> Four Calling Birds
> Three French Hens
> Two Turtle Doves
> and a Partridge in a Pear Tree.

The hams, mostly in the men's sportswear and suits department would hold out the last note as long as they could. It was funny, at least for a short while since Jeff and Gary had such horrid voices.

The big Christmas shopping surge, and the twenty-four hour plus sale at the store was well advertised. Many retailers had their entire season riding on that short period from Thanksgiving night until midnight on Friday. Many stores felt that if they didn't make it now then they would have to close down after the holidays. The Big B wasn't one of them but the other store that began with a B, which no one was allowed to mention inside of the department store, had already announced that it was done. Competition was fierce and Mr. B was not one to lose. He had thrown everything he could at these few hours that started the holiday selling season. There were deep discounts every hour on big ticket items. The As Seen on TV section featured wonderfully, useless items that no one could live without. The Eggstractor was a priceless item that would go on sale that night for one time only. Adam would demonstrate it to the joy of happy, grinning faces every hour on the hour as buyers would watch the hardboiled eggs lose their hard shell to display shining, glistening, edible, egg delights. No doubt this was an important night for all the co-workers. None of them wanted to let Mr. B, or Pat down.

The weatherman wasn't cooperating with Mr. B's big plans to keep the store open all night. In fact, the prediction was for the worst winter storm of the century with below freezing cold and snow stacked to the ceiling. The prediction was for a monumental blast that came down from Canada, without a visa, over the Great Lakes while it gathered moisture and then dumped several feet of snow fast and hard on areas of Western Pennsylvania. It was going to be bad, but like all retail people, they had to be there for those crazy people who would start their Christmas shopping in order to get those one of a kind deals. They all knew the phrase, "If it says Crazy Prices, then you'd be crazy not to buy it." Gay and Gail in the Christmas Department came in dressed as two of Santa's little elves. Both were overjoyed at the start of this bustling season and flitted around the store handing out candy canes to all the workers.

Shortly after six, the storm rolled in, or rather, it attacked Clearview Mall and the surrounding town. It fell quick and it fell deep. By 6:30 pm, it was obvious that no one would be shopping and the co-workers that were in the store would be there until morning. The State Police had closed the roads and no one was to go out, irregardless of the emergency. The manager, Pat, decided to keep the doors open in an optimistic hope that a customer would walk in but since dogsleds were rarely used in Butler, it was an optimistic dirigible of hope that would soon crash and burn.

For the first hour, co-workers gathered around the registers in their departments, joking and laughing. Every few minutes, crazy Ella would race outside, swear a foul string of nasty words at the snow, and measure the accumulation total. It would be reported by Jessie over the store speakers to moans and frustrated exclamations. It would be a long, uneventful night. No one could get in and only the smokers could get out but not very far. There was a constantly shoveled pathway that allowed them minimal movement in a small, snow enclosed area. It didn't matter, no one was going too far in the frigid cold anyway.

The flakes fell large, heavy and wet. The rest of the mall had closed at the threat of the record breaking storm. The Big B held to its principles. It was there to serve their customers. Through rain, through sleet and through one helluva snow storm those crazy prices with up to 80% off items in the Auditorium would wait for customers.

Gay and Gail kept their door open in hopes of some wandering Eskimo. They even pulled out some of the summer furniture for them. Gay thought it seemed more like summer for an Alaskan so she would be prepared. As a top manager and acute, and a cute, marketing mind, she would be ready for all customers.

By nine pm, everyone was walking around the store, talking and making jokes about where to sleep and who to sleep with. They found Vicki's white lab coat hanging on the Men's Department dressing room door. It was a game to guess who else was in there. Most of the other co-workers assembled in the furniture department. The Candyman, had popped open a few tins of popcorn and it was passing around the furniture department. Susanna scolded him, "Tony, that popcorn is coming out of your pay!"

Tony's response was typical for him. "Send the bill to my ex-wife." Later, even she was laughing by the end of the first can passing. Controlling Tony, the Candyman, was like herding cats. Garry was insistent that no one touch the upholstery with greasy hands but his appeals fell on mostly laughing faces and deaf ears. It wasn't long before he, too was sitting in the middle of the group telling dog show and

Chapter 1: A Parted Head in a Pear Tree

Everyone had thought it was a bad idea from the beginning. Sure, Kohl's was stealing business by staying open twenty-four hours but most of the employees didn't want time stolen from their families. Here it was, Thanksgiving Night and the store opened at six pm and would stay open all the way through Black Friday till the early hours of Saturday. That was retail. Everyone who worked retail knew it was murder for the next month. None of them thought, though, that it would be murder, literally.

The management of the store did their best to

a bunch about your character in the book. Speaking of characters, I didn't have enough room to get everyone in the book. I did think about you. I tried to imagine you at home relaxing while all the others were getting knocked-off one by one. If there is ever a sequel then you can assured you will be in it.

I want to thank the many of you who became friends. I see the store as a village. Everyone has been a character in the village. I was welcomed and soon found friends that made each day passable and enjoyable. Just make sure the village idiot has some fudge ready for me whenever I return.

A final thank you to Stacy Merrison who drew the cover and added illustrations. I wasn't sure that everyone could read so we added pictures for those in the furniture and men's departments.